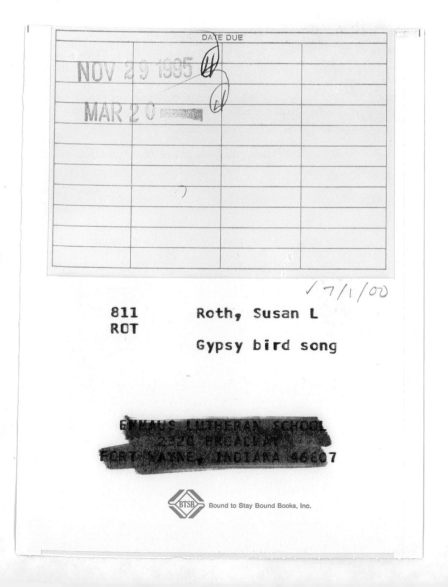

GYPSY BIRD SONG

SUSAN L. ROTH

FARRAR STRAUS GIROUX
NEW YORK

FOR PETER FOR NANCY

Copyright © 1991 by Susan L. Roth
All rights reserved
Library of Congress catalog card number: 90-27210
Published simultaneously in Canada by HarperCollins *Canada Ltd*
Color separations by Imago Publishing Ltd.
Printed and bound in the United States of America
Designed by Martha Rago
First edition, 1991

Whenever you see a Gypsy Bird,
it means the gypsies are near.
                              —*Old Gypsy Saying*

Shake your tail,
Gypsy Bird, so I
really know it's you and not some other pipit.
Show your clashing colors, Gypsy Bird.
Dazzle my eyes and prove you're not
just any old land bird.
Walk your straight, proud walk
like a gypsy, Gypsy Bird,
with that touch of swagger,
so I see without a squint it's you
and not your brother.
Head up and wink your eye, Gypsy Bird.
Point those piebald feathers, Pied Wagtail that you are,
and chirp me your legend:
The gypsies are near,
The gypsies are near!

My little house
is our traveling wagon,
with fringe on the doorway,
green stripes above it,
pink stripes below it;
flowery curtains,
lace on the edges,
rickrack and ruffles;
embroidered-on lamp shades,
beads on the tatting;
boxes of flowers
painted on both sides,
stars on the outside,
dots on the topside,
zigzags beneath them;
mirrors on our quilting,
sewn into the fabric;
skirts on the bed,
the chair,
the table;
red ceiling and red walls
under the frame that's
surrounding the picture
of our traveling wagon,
which is
my little house.

The wagons are loaded,
the horses are ready,
we're off to the market!
We've washed our faces,
we've eaten breakfast,
we're off to the market!
While Papa sells
his pots, his pans,
while he's trading, buying,
while Mama sits,
telling her fortunes,
looking at futures,
while Uncle grinds
his knives, his music,
then I'll fetch the water,
I'll feed the horses,
I'll help with the cooking.
I won't even be tired
when we get to the market.
I can't wait to get there!
Do we have to go farther?
How much longer?
How much longer?—laughs Papa.
We only just started.
But we're going!
We're off to the market!

Tinker tinker
hammer hammer
bash the tin
make it flatter.
Knock knock
tinkle tinkle
hear the sounds
of Papa's hammer.
Bink bink
rattle rattle
plink plink
tattle tattle
tink tink
listen to him
never stopping
with his tinning.
Papa's fixing his pots, his pans.
He can do anything with his hands.

We look for marshy places
near the forest edge
where the reeds grow wild.
In the grassy bogs
we gather the reeds.
We bring them to camp,
to dry them out.
When they're dry
we bunch them together,
we braid them fine.
Our fingers push-pull,
sometimes they bleed,
but we weave those reeds,
forwards,
backwards,
in,
out,
up,
down,
all around,
like stars,
like snowflakes,
like webs,
like flowers,
never forgetting the order of things.
By the end of the day
there are baskets;
many sizes, many shapes,
some to keep, some to use,
some to sell in the market.

That's my uncle,
the organ-grinder.
He cranks his old wooden instrument.
It's a wooden box of hammers and holes.
It sits on stilts
which stand on wheels
so it can move
when my uncle moves.
It leaks music.
It knocks, it wheezes out
crooked melodies
one after another.

My uncle's monkey
wears a little suit.
He paces up and down
on the ground,
his little cap
in his little hand,
waiting for coins.

When the music stops,
he gets his piece of bread.
The monkey sits
on top of the organ.
Then the organ-grinder, that's my uncle,
pushes off
for a new corner of the market.

Papa says it's the bad bargainers
who give gypsies their bad name.
Am I a cheater? asks Papa.
He holds his big hands out,
open for me to see.
Gypsies don't cheat, like those bad sports say.
We're just doing our jobs.
We bargain like the professionals
that we are.
Those sore losers wish they'd win,
but they can't come out ahead of us.
They lack the technique, the polish.
They don't have the gypsy touch.
That's our luck.
If they pay too much silver
for a piece of bad gold, am I to blame?
They need to know how much the gold is worth
before they start to dicker.
They need to know who it is they're dealing with.
Is it my fault they don't know how to bargain? Is it?

No, I say. I'm feeling proud now.
Teach me how to bargain like a gypsy, Papa.
But Papa smiles and says I don't need lessons.
It's all there inside you, Little One,
in your gypsy blood.

"Three silver coins," whispers the pointy-nosed girl
as she shakes them from her sleeve
into Mama's open hand.
"Three silver coins," says Mama.
She starts to read her crystal ball
with a black-eyed stare.
She doesn't blink.
Long and happy life, she says.
Good husband, she says.
Pretty children, she says.
Gold enough so you won't be hungry, she says.
Then her eyelids go down like window shades
on a storefront at closing time.

Mama hooks up the heavy kettle
full of water to let it boil, but
I can do the rest.

First you put in onions, if you haven't any leeks.
If you have some garlic,
cut the pieces small.
Watch your fingers.
Next for turnips, with their greens;
wild dill if you're in Greece,
fennel if you're in Sicily,
paprika if you're in Hungary;
then the chicken.
You can't have too many chickens
nor too few.
If you're by the sea, use fish.
If you're in Turkey, use goat.
Take your great big spoon, stir.
If some water disappears,
add a little more.
If you have rosemary or thyme,
throw it in the pot.
If you're in Ireland, use potatoes.
Don't forget the carrots.

Now there's time to tend the horses.

When the dill starts filling up the air,
when the stew starts to smell so good,
when you just can't wait another minute,
taste the broth.
Add the salt.
Wait a little longer.
Get the bowls all ready,
in a pile.

Then call your papa, call
your mama. Call your sisters,
call your brothers. Chase the dogs
away till later.
Ladle out your stew.
Eat.

When I hear Papa's black violin
I hear him call my name.
His voice is music to my ears.
Gypsy, Little Gypsy,
get up to dance, he sings.
His bow arm
pulls my feet
from under my skirts.
Turning, turning,
I begin to dance as I see
flowers pour out from the F holes,
but

in the middle of my spin
the music changes.
His black violin begins to wail.
It sobs,
it slows my feet.
My skirts unfurl.
My arms drop.
I droop.
Yet

in the middle of my fall
he has a change of heart again.
Suddenly
his bow arm moves so fast
I can't see it.
His music ribbons
stripe the air red,
yellow, blue,
green.
As colors fly from the black violin
I can't remember even a hint
of sad song.

I have ears, feet
only for the voice
of Papa's black violin.

The diklo,
the gypsy scarf,
the gypsy mark,
it's a piece of silk,
a little square,
a thousand colors,
a kaleidoscope.
It waves on the neck
when it's tied,
first under,
then over,
in the precise way
that only gypsies can do.

The diklo,
the gypsy scarf,
it's only a gypsy
who wears that flag.
If you ever see
a diklo around the neck of
not-a-gypsy,
then you may be sure
this is a special person,
a friend who has received a gift
from a real gypsy.
You must treat the
not-a-gypsy
like a gypsy.

My arms are full of
clanking bangles,
gold and silver shining
bangles, bonking clacking
jingling jangles
knocking, tinkling
clinking dangles,
eighteen jangling
mingling jingles,
every single tinkling
tingle, knocking
bonking clinking
ringing
clanking bangles,
eighteen gold and silver bangles
jingling on my arms

Bent twig,
whisper us our secret,
give us our
for-our-eyes-only
message.
Point us in our right direction.
To anyone else
you may be just a bent twig, but
you're the world to us.
You're the map, waiting patient
till we come along.
Chart the way,
left or right,
at the fork,
if we're lost.
Bent twig, you're the marker.
Don't you move till we get to you.
Don't let the wind or anything else
push you aside
and change your twig-sign.
If when we're lost we read you wrong,
we could be lost forever.
But if we read you right,
if we follow you,
we'll be safe; we'll get home,
wherever home is,
tonight.

Orange shadows
dancing with the bushes
in the hushed-up
night light.
Fire's
flying high, flapping,
snapping in the wind in the
night light.

It's the gypsies
watching flames
watching smoke
watching shadows,
scary gypsies
leaning on the trees.
What's that walking on the roof
of our wagon? It's in the sky!
It's in the night light.
See the
shadows painting orange
on the floor
in the forest? It's the
gypsies, yes, the gypsies
in the night light.
See the spitting
at the pines in the night? But
where's the moon?
I think it's gone!
See the shadows
moving on?
Now it's orange
now it's brown
what was that?
It's just the wind
or maybe shadows,
or the fire, snapping,
smoking.
It's the gypsies,
in the what?
In the night light.

When the Big Fat Moon Man
sits sideways in the sky,
it's like I could touch him.
He doesn't do much lighting up
when he sits like that, he
only makes the gypsies talk.
"Look at that Moon Man,"
"Old Orange-Face is so low,"
"See the Moon tonight"
is what they say.
I put my arms around his Big Fat Neck.
"Tell me your secret"—he shines at me—
"and I'll tell you mine."
I whisper
into his Big Fat Orange Ear.
He whispers softly back to me.
Then slowly, slowly he slips off.
He loses his color
and he rises.

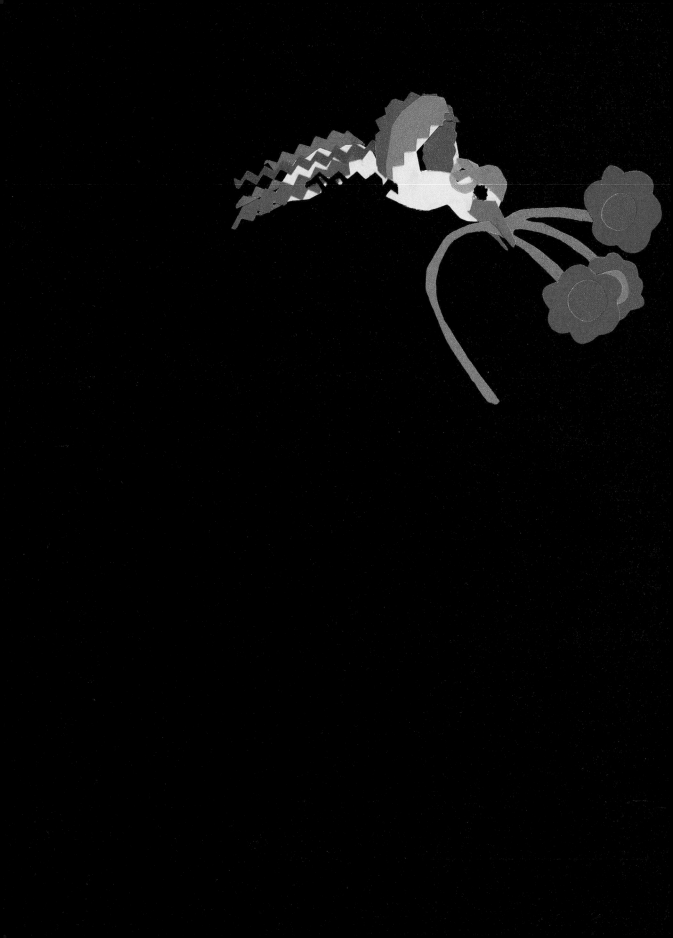